THE TALKING TREE

(AN OLD ITALIAN TALE)

RETOLD BY INNA RAYEVSKY
ILLUSTRATED BY ROBERT RAYEVSKY

G. P. PUTNAM'S SONS
NEW YORK

The text for this version of *The Talking Tree* has been adapted from a story
of the same name in *The Talking Tree, Fairy Tales from 15 Lands*, selected by
Augusta Baker, and published by J. B. Lippincott Company.

G. P. Putnam's Sons, a division of The Putnam & Grosset Group,
200 Madison Avenue, New York, NY 10016.
Published simultaneously in Canada. Printed in Hong Kong by
South China Printing Co. (1988) Ltd. Book design by Vladimir Radunsky.

Library of Congress Cataloging-in-Publication Data
Rayevsky, Inna. The talking tree.
Summary: A king's search for the fabulous Talking Tree leads him to
risk his life trying to release an enchanted princess from a witch's spell.
[1. Fairy tales. 2. Folklore—Italy] I. Rayevsky, Robert, ill. II. Title.
PZ8.R339Tal 1989 398.2'1'0945 [E] 88-32105 ISBN 0-399-21631-6
1 3 5 7 9 10 8 6 4 2
First Impression

With thanks to Betty Schwartz—I. R. and R. R.

Once upon a time there was a king who fancied he had collected in his palace all the rarest things in the world.

One day a stranger came and asked permission to see the collection. He observed everything minutely, and then said, "May it please Your Majesty, but the best thing of all is missing."

"Missing! What is missing?" demanded the king.

"The Talking Tree," replied the stranger.

"A Talking Tree!" exclaimed the king. "But where can one find such an oddity?"

"I no longer remember," answered the stranger, "but I have seen it in a forest with my own eyes and I have heard it with my own ears."

"And what exactly did it say?" inquired the king.

"It said:

'Ever to wait for what never comes,
Is enough to give one the worst doldrums!'

"Amazing!" said the king, his head now spinning from the desire to have this tree in his collection. "I shall see to this matter at once!"

He clapped his hands, he stomped his foot, and immediately messengers and exploring commissions were sent to all the forests of the world in search of the Talking Tree.

But as the days and months went by, the messengers returned empty-handed.

"You are good for nothing!" roared the king. "I shall go and find the Talking Tree myself! And woe to the stranger if his story is not true!"

So the very next morning the king set out in disguise for his long journey. He walked and walked, and at last found himself in a deep forest where not one living soul was to be seen. Exhausted, he chose a beautiful tree with lush, gently swaying branches, and stretched himself out on the ground beneath it.

Just as he was dropping off to sleep, he heard a voice as if someone were weeping:

"Ever to wait for what never comes,
      Is enough to give one the worst doldrums!"

The words were exactly those of the Talking Tree!

"This must be it!" thought the startled king, and to make sure, he reached up and plucked a leaf from the tree.

"Oh, why do you hurt me so!" said a sad voice.

Now the king became quite terrified in spite of all his daring, yet he asked, "Who are you? If you are a living soul, in the name of heaven, answer me!"

"I am a princess," said the voice. "One day I saw a fountain as clear as crystal and thought I would bathe in it, but as soon as I touched its waters I turned into a tree. It was an old witch's trap!"

"Poor creature!" exclaimed the king. "What can I do to set you free?"

"It is not that simple," the voice replied. "You must cut me down with the magic axe that belongs to the cruel ogre, you must kill the horrible witch, and you must swear to marry me."

"I swear! I swear!" promised the king. "And I shall find the axe even if I have to go to the ends of the earth!"

"Yes," sighed the tree, "but now hide yourself, the witch is coming!"

The king hid himself behind a bush nearby, and saw the witch come riding on her broomstick.

"To whom were you talking?" demanded the witch.

"To the wind that blows," answered the tree.

"But I see footprints here!"

"They may be your own."

"Ah, they're mine, are they?" cried the enraged witch. And seizing her broomstick, she struck the tree, over and over, screaming all the while, "Liar! They're mine, are they? Wait till I get you!"

The king was greatly distressed at this, but as he could do nothing, he resolved to go and find the magic axe.

He began to retrace his steps, but he took the wrong path and again found himself quite lost in the midst of a thick wood.

"Which way should I go *now?*" despaired the king.

When suddenly, he saw in front of him a beautiful young girl!

"Lovely maiden," said the surprised king, "for charity's sake, show me how I may get out of these woods. I have lost my way."

"Ah, poor fellow, however did you get here? My father, the ogre, will come by shortly and he will eat you up alive, you poor soul!"

And no sooner did she say this, then they heard a deafening noise that rang through the whole forest. It was the ogre himself coming home with his hundred mastiffs barking and yelping at his heels.

"Now I am lost for good!" thought the king in horror.

"Come here!" cried the maiden. "Throw yourself flat down, and I shall cover you with my skirts. Don't even breathe!"

When the ogre saw his daughter, he stopped.

"What a fine smell of human flesh!" he roared.

"A little boy went past, and I gobbled him up."

"Well done! And his bones?"

"The dogs ate them."

"Oh, how hungry I am!" thundered the ogre, and calling his dogs, he disappeared into the forest.

When the ogre had gone off, the king came out of his hiding place and told his whole story to the kind maiden.

"If Your Majesty will but promise to marry me, I can give you the axe you are looking for," said the girl.

"Alas, fair maiden, I have already pledged my word!"

"That's unlucky for me. But no matter," said the girl, smiling slyly,

and she led the king to a great mansion that belonged to her father.

"Is this what you need?" she asked with a twinkle in her eye, as she handed the king a mighty-looking axe.

"Yes, yes!" said the king. "But what is this grease on the edge?"

"It is just some oil from the whetstone on which it was sharpened," the girl replied hastily.

No sooner had the king touched the axe, he was back at the spot where the Talking Tree stood. The witch was not there, so the tree said to him, "Now that you have the axe, take care! My heart is hidden away in the trunk. If the witch tells you to strike high up, you must strike down. If she tells you to strike down, you must strike up— or else you will kill me! And do not forget to cut the nasty old witch's head off with one blow, or she will put a spell on you too!"

As the tree finished its words, the witch appeared again.

"What are you looking for in these parts?" she asked the king suspisciously.

"I am looking for a tree to make charcoal," answered the king.

"Take this one! Take this one!" shrieked the witch, pointing to the Talking Tree. "Just strike exactly where I tell you and it's all yours!"

But the king pretended to miss.

"Oh, I am sorry!" he said. "Let me try again; a bright star in the sky distracted me."

"A star? By daylight? That's impossible!" shouted the witch. And as she turned her back to look up, the king aimed a mighty blow and cut her head clean off.

Thus the enchantment was broken, and from the trunk of the tree there stepped forth a princess so lovely that one could scarcely look at her. The king, delighted at having saved her, brought her back to his palace and ordered splendid rejoicings and preparations for the celebration of their wedding. stop

When the day came and the court ladies were dressing the princess in her bridal robes, to their great astonishment they perceived that she was made of . . . wood! One of them flew to the king.

"Your Majesty, the princess is not of flesh and blood but of wood!"

The king and his ministers raced to see this wonder. To sight the princess was like a living woman—anyone would have been deceived— but to the touch she was indeed wood.

The ministers declared that the king could not marry a wooden doll, even though it could talk and move.

"There still must be some other spell hanging over her!" cried the king in his frustration. And then he remembered the grease on the axe. He took a piece of meat and cut it with the axe. Sure enough, the meat looked like meat, but to the touch it was wood! So it was the ogre's daughter who had betrayed him through her jealousy!

"I must see her at once!" said the king. And since he still had the magic axe, his wish was granted immediately. Once more he found himself at the home of the ogre, where to his good fortune, only the daughter was at home.

"Here is the axe you lent me, lovely maiden," said the king to her. And in giving the axe to her the king contrived to prick her hand with the point.

"Ah! What has Your Majesty done to me?" cried the maiden. "I am turning into wood!"

The king pretended to be much grieved.

"Is there no remedy for it?" he asked.

"Yes!" she cried. "Open that cupboard, and in it you will find a pot of ointment. Rub it on me and I shall be cured at once!"

The king took the pot of ointment, but instead dashed out with it and cried, "Now wait till I come back!"

The ogre's daughter understood, but too late.

"Catch him! Catch him!" she screamed, as she unleashed the ogre's mastiffs.

Yet it was all of no use, for the king was already far away.

So the lovely princess was finally freed from the spell and returned to her natural state; and as she was no longer a wooden doll, the ministers agreed to the wedding celebration.

And what a grand celebration it was! With such dancing, feasting and merrymaking that everybody remembered it for a very long time.